Spot Goes to the Park

Eric Hill

Let's all go to
It's so nice

the park, Spot.
today.

Come on, Spot.

Wait for us,

Helen! Spot! the

Don't chase pigeons!

Oops!
Where did the
ball go?

Spot likes
the swing.

Who is
Spot waving to?

Now Spot and play piggy- with Tom.

Helen
in- the-middle

Look! The ball is coming back to Spot!

What
Say "thank

a kind duck.
you," Spot.

Quack, quack!

PUFFIN BOOKS

Published by the Penguin Group: London, New York,
Australia, Canada, India, New Zealand and South Africa
Penguin Books Ltd, Registered Offices:
80 Strand, London WC2R 0RL, England

www.penguin.com

First published by William Heinemann Ltd, 1991
Published in Puffin Books 1993
21 23 25 27 29 30 28 26 24 22

Printed and bound in Malaysia

ISBN 0–140–54909-9